SCOOBY-DOO!
SEA MONSTER SCARE

By Gail Herman

Illustrated by Duendes del Sur

SCHOLASTIC INC.

New York   Toronto   London   Auckland   Sydney
Mexico City   New Delhi   Hong Kong   Buenos Aires

ISBN 0-439-31831-9

25 24 23 22 21 20   08 09 10 11/0

Printed in the U.S.A.
First Scholastic printing, May 2002

It was a perfect day for the beach. "Ret's ro!" Scooby-Doo said to his friends.

"Scoob is right," Shaggy said. "Surf's up!"

3

Velma pulled a wagon. It was filled with shovels and pails and flags. "I'm ready to make a one-of-a-kind sand castle!" she said.

Scooby pulled another wagon. It was filled with sandwiches and pizza, hot dogs, and tons of chips.

"We're ready for a one-of-a-kind lunch!" Shaggy said.

"This is a good spot!" said Velma. She took everything from the wagon. Then she filled the pails with sand. Fred turned them over. And Daphne lifted them up.

"This sand castle will be perfect!" said Velma.

6

"Mmm-mmm! This sandwich is perfect," said Shaggy.

Scooby and Shaggy ate their way through piles of food. Finally, they burped.

"Like, we're all done!" said Shaggy.

"Us too," said Velma.

Shaggy and Scooby looked over. Their
jaws dropped. "Holy cow!" said Shaggy.
The castle had moats and bridges, and
winding steps. Flags flew from towers.
"It is good," Velma agreed.
"Like, I'm not talking about the castle,"
said Shaggy. "We're out of food!"

"Out of food?" Daphne laughed.

"And we didn't have a bite!" said Fred.

Scooby hung his head. "Rorry."

"Sorry," Shaggy echoed. "How about Scoob and I make a food run? There's a Snack Shack down the beach!"

Scooby and Shaggy set off. A little while later, they were back. At least, they thought they were.

They saw the blanket. They saw Velma's book. But that was all.

"Zoinks!" said Shaggy. "Everyone has disappeared! And so has the sand castle!"

All around them, people snatched up
blankets. They threw books, bottles of
sunscreen, and other things into beach bags.
They rushed away.

"Something horrible has happened!" cried
Shaggy. "We need clues!"

Scooby gazed out to sea. "Rook!" he gasped.
A giant sea serpent rode the waves.
"Like, that thing did it!" said Shaggy. "It took
the sand castle, *and* the gang!"

Shouts rang out across the water.
"It's getting closer!" Shaggy cried.
Scooby yelped, "Run, Raggy!"

The buddies took off. They jumped over people. They scooted around umbrellas. But the sea serpent was close behind.

It was coming onto the beach!

"A surfboard, Scoob!" Shaggy shouted. "Quick! Hop on!"

A moment later, they bounced along the waves. "Like, hang ten, Scoob!" Shaggy said.

But they couldn't surf fast enough. The monster was closing in!

The sea grew rough. Scooby and Shaggy hung on. Wave after wave. Up, down. Up, down.

Scooby turned green. "Don't lose
your lunch, good buddy," Shaggy said.
Up, down. Up, down.
Shaggy turned green too.

All at once, a giant wave crashed
over them. Shaggy clung to Scooby.
Scooby clung to Shaggy.
Whoosh!

Up, up, up they went. The surfboard
went one way. Scooby and Shaggy
went the other way.

They hung in the air. Then they dropped —
fast. Right onto the back of the sea serpent!

"Help!" "Relp!" they cried.
"Don't worry," said Velma. "We're
right here."
Scooby spun around. Velma,
Fred, and Daphne were on the
serpent's back, too.

"We've got to get off!"
Shaggy screamed.
"Relax," said Fred.
"The ride will be over
soon."

"Ride?" said Shaggy. "The serpent gives rides?"
"It's not a real monster," said Daphne. "It's a
float."
Scooby and Shaggy gazed around. People were
laughing and having fun.

"But what about the people on the beach?"
asked Shaggy. "Why did they run away? And
what about the sand castle? I thought a monster wiped it out."

"The sand castle is gone?" Velma gasped.

Then she sighed. "It must have been the tide. That's what happens with sand castles. The tide sweeps them away. And those people? They were only moving away from the water."

The monster float stopped with a bump. They were back at their spot at the beach.

"Like, forget the sand castle," said Shaggy. "All our food has been swept away, too!"

"Rack Rack?" said Scooby.

"Snack Shack!" agreed Shaggy.

Scooby-dooby-doo!